Night at the Museum

∧

George W. Bush Presidential

RON BRACKIN

New York Times best-selling author of *Son of Hamas*

ISBN-13: 978-0692283479
Cover Art and illustrations by Ethan Brackin

ADDITIONAL TITLES:

- Sherlock Holmes: The Adventure of the Deadly Illusion
- Sweet Persecution
- "I forgive you. Pass it on!"
- A closer look at Love
- Chats with my Beloved
- Dracula: A Devotional
- Oliver Twist: A Devotional
- Much Ado about Nothing: A Devotional

Table of Contents

Introduction

The George W. Bush Presidential Museum opened May 1, 2013.

But long before its cornerstone had been laid, before the Rangers had won their first American League Championship, or JFK had been assassinated in Dealey Plaza ...

Before the Second World War, the Great Depression, or the Spanish-American War ... really, really long ago, Caddo Indians lived on the land we call Texas.

People who know about such things say ancestors of the Caddo hunted and farmed here as far back as ten thousand years before the birth of Jesus Christ. They hunted and farmed here while Egyptians quarried millions of tons of granite and limestone to build the Great Pyramid of Cheops.

Around 800 A.D., many started calling themselves

Kaduhdaachu (Kah-DA-da DA-choo), which, over the years wore away to *Caddo*.

The Caddo hunted and farmed …
while the Mayan Empire collapsed,
while William the Conqueror invaded England,
throughout the inglorious Crusades.

They planted corn and beans and squash and wove baskets out of strips of cane and made wooden tools. Caddo potters created beautiful bowls and bottles that looked as though they had been fashioned out of dark chocolate. They built beehive-shaped lodges that often stood fifty feet high and sixty feet wide, where as many as twenty men, women and children lived and gathered together around a central fire and slept snugly on their beds under buffalo robes and deerskins. They hunted and fished and loved one another and married one another and had children.

One of those children was a boy named Kaaytsi, which means Owl in our language. His parents named him Screech Owl because he screeched when he was a baby and he continued to screech as a boy at play. But the bighorn sheep and puma and peccary, the kangaroo rat, skink and hare, the alligator and the armadillo all called him Little Owl. And since everybody knows that animals can sometimes be wiser than people, everyone else began to call him Little Owl too. His mother only called him Kaaytsi when he was being particularly troublesome, which has been the way of mothers since Eve.

Little Owl lived with his parents, three brothers and two sisters in a village on the Red River. And that's where our story begins. On the Red River, really, really long ago …

Chapter One

L ittle Owl was like you and me, except that he never had to dress up in uncomfortable clothes for special occasions. Also, he didn't go to school, because there was no such thing. But he still had to learn a lot of things, just as we do.

More than just about anything, Little Owl loved to hunt and fish. He also loved to eat. His favorite meal was porridge, because his mother sweetened it with fresh, ripe blackberries.

Porridge and berries were also a favorite of a mystical, magical, mischievous rascal named Coyote, who often stole Little Owl's porridge and disappeared before the boy could reach for his bow and arrows.

One day, Little Owl decided to pull a prank on Coyote. He picked a handful of green ground cherries, which are the color of butterscotch when they're ripe and ready to eat. But if you eat ground cherries before they're ripe, they will make your stomach churn like storm clouds.

At supper that evening, Little Owl's mother filled his bowl with porridge as usual. But when she gave him a handful of blackberries, Little Owl replaced them with the green ground cherries.

You can probably guess what happened next, and of course you'd be right.

Before Little Owl could even pick up his spoon, Coyote appeared out of thin air, grabbed the bowl, gobbled down the porridge and was gone. He had just disappeared, which was one of his mystical, magical powers.

Where the thief had stood, there was only the sound of spitting and groaning. Then, slowly, the doubled-over form of Coyote began to reappear.

"Arghhh!" He croaked, squeezing his stomach. "Kaaytsi!" He shouted. "You poisoned me!"

"You poisoned yourself," laughed Little Owl. "But don't worry, Coyote, you're not going to die, even if that were possible. But you're going to be awfully, awfully sick!"

And Little Owl rolled on his back and laughed even harder, kicking his feet in the air like a puppy that wants its belly scratched.

Suddenly, Coyote stopped groaning as anger overcame his cramp.

Little owl looked up.

Coyote's eyes blazed. His fur bristled. His claws quivered. And his sharp teeth glistened in a terrifying snarl.

Little Owl's big, soft eyes grew even bigger.

Quick as summer lighting, the boy sprang to his feet and raced for his weapons, with Coyote at his heels.

Coyote howled something the boy could not understand. Sounds that rhymed, a little like a chant, but with the authority of a command.

Little Owl dove for his bow, reached for his arrows … and found himself with a bow in one hand and a fistful of grass in the other. He looked up.

Then, he looked around.

Coyote was gone.

His mother and father and brothers and sisters were gone The lodge and the village we're gone.

Even his beautiful Red River was gone.

Little Owl was all alone.

He looked this way and that way. But all he could see in any direction was tall prairie grass, moving lazily in the wind like waves of an edgeless sea.

Have you ever visited a shopping mall and seen the big signs that show you where all the shops are, and there's a red arrow somewhere on the sign that says, "YOU ARE HERE"? The mall owners include the arrow because they know that, in order for us to get where we're *going*, we first need to know where we *are*. And Little Owl had no idea where he was.

Everywhere he looked, everything looked the same.

So, he started walking.

It was no use looking at the sun to see if he was walking in the right direction, because he didn't know whether he had landed (if that's the right word) north, south, east or west of his village on the Red River.

But it had occurred to him that, if he walked long enough in any direction, he was bound to reach the rim of the prairie and discover something familiar that would help him find his way home.

So he walked.

And he walked.

And he walked, for days. Then weeks. But he could never seem to get free of the Prairie.

After walking a whole month, Little Owl realized that Coyote had put a spell on him and that he really hadn't walked anywhere at all. He was right where he had started.

Coyote had magically banished Little Owl to a distant prairie, and here he would stay unless he could find a way to break the spell.

"I'll try until I die," he declared to no one in particular. And he thought about his mother and father and brothers and sisters and the bighorn sheep and puma and peccary, the kangaroo rat, skink and hare, the alligator and the armadillo.

And maybe he cried a little

I would have. Wouldn't you?

As moons grew full and waned, Little Owl tried everything he could think of to break Coyote's spell.

He tried, as seasons chased one another in circles.

He tried, as men came in ships from Europe, Spain and France. Missionaries and explorers. Trappers, traders and settlers.

He tried, as wars came and went, and more wars came. Wars between Indians. Wars between white men and Indians. Wars between white men. Endless, horrible wars.

Years became decades.

Decades became centuries.

But Little Owl just remained Little Owl. Never growing older. Never becoming a warrior. Never marrying and teaching sons to hunt and care for the land and become brave and honorable.

But he never stopped trying.

The prairie vanished. Farms and villages, towns and cities rose up out of the clay, fell to ruin, and blew away like tumbleweeds.

Amazing changes happened, faster and faster and closer together. Sometimes Little Owl found it hard to breathe, not just because the air was no longer pure and sweet, but because of the exhausting speed of change.

People moved fast. Machines that replaced horses

moved fast. Air machines streaked across the skies like shooting stars.

Throughout centuries, Little Owl had many adventures as he continued to search for a way home. And as would be expected, many of those adventures involved unpleasant encounters with Coyote.

But he never stopped trying.

Someday, somewhere, he told himself again and again, he would find something that had the power to break the curse and return him to his family.

You see, Little Owl believed there is a spirit in everything—not just in people, but in animals, trees and even rocks. And spirits have power. Some have GREAT power. Others have so little power that it's almost as though they have none at all.

Coyote had great power But surely, Little Owl thought, there must be something that has greater power. And he was determined to find it.

Coyote was just as determined that he wouldn't.

Many, many times, Little Owl discovered an object he thought might be strong enough to break the spell. But Coyote nearly always reached it first and hid it. Or, if Little Owl did manage to get his hands on it, Coyote stole it. Sometimes, they reached it at the same time and struggled over it. Then, Coyote would cheat with his mystical, magical powers.

What Coyote often seemed to forget, however, is that objects of great power are often objects of great virtue as well. And whenever Coyote touched one of these, he had cause to regret it, because virtue and mischief do not mix. Sometimes, Coyote got zapped as if by lightning. Other times, the object burned his paws. One time, an object of power and virtue cause his bones to rattle when he moved, so, for the longest time, he found it almost impossible to sneak up on anybody, including deer and cottontails and ground squirrels. And, since coyotes eat deer and cottontails and ground squirrels, he grew very, very hungry.

None of the objects, though, had enough power to set Little Owl free.

Then, one day, he found himself in the lodge of a very great chief.

"Surely," he thought, "my exile is about to end."

Chapter Two

The limestone was cool under Little Owl's bare feet. The museum was quiet at night, except for the muted sounds of uniformed security officers keeping watch and the occasional crackle of a walkie talkie. High-definition monitors revealed anything that moved.

Just then, as an officer stared at the monitors, a shadow—really more like the shadow of a shadow —drifted across one of the screens. But the officer saw nothing.

Nor did Little Owl.

He had no idea that Coyote was stalking the museum gallery in search of anything that threatened to break his hold over Little Owl.

Like bullies everywhere, Coyote believed that force was the only real power. So it was little wonder that he paused in front of a display case that featured a nasty-looking black gun.

"This," he thought, *"might be just the thing that will enable that wretched boy to break my spell."*

A label read:

9mm Glock Model 18C Automatic Pistol, confiscated from Saddam Hussein during his capture on December 13, 2003. Members of the U.S. Army's 1st Brigade Combat Team from the 4th Infantry Division presented the framed gun to President Bush on March 1, 2004.

Coyote couldn't help himself. He just had to touch it. He needed to feel the cold steel, thrill at the weight of it in his hand … and he had to hide it where Little Owl could never find it.

Coyote reached into the display case and touched the pistol, petting it like a child with a gerbil.

Suddenly, as though he had rubbed a magic lamp, there was a loud CRACK! and a belch of oily, black smoke. And before him stood a rat. Not a little rat, like the ones you see in New York City or Paris. This rat was BIG! It's skin was scaly where patches of hair were missing. The fur on its head was bushy. And it had a bushy beard, not at all like New York or Paris rats. And there were baggy, saggy bags under its beady black eyes.

"Sssaddam," hissed the rat, "at your ssservice."

Coyote had heard snakes hiss in the desert, but the rats he had eaten had only squeaked or squealed. None had ever hissed. Nevertheless, I am assured by the most reliable sources that rats do indeed hiss on occasion. This rat, however, seemed to do it habitually, and Coyote immediately found it annoying.

Saddam stood on his hind legs and rocked back and forth on his heels, steadying himself with his tail, like a kangaroo.

This annoyed Coyote, too.

The rat smiled. A wicked, distasteful smile. And when it smiled, a gap appeared where a long sharp front tooth should have been.

"Well," Coyote thought, *"no wonder it hisses."*

"Why did you pet the gun?" Saddam asked, as he groomed himself with a greasy, grey tongue.

"That's none of your concern," said Coyote, growing even more annoyed. "Go back to where you came from."

"I can't," said the rat, "because you ssummoned me. I was sstuck in my pisstol until ssomeone came who would gaze at the gun with fondness insstead of dissgusst. Command me."

"Command you to do what?"

"Whatever you wish. You could sstart by telling me why you're here. Perhapss I can be of asssissstance."

Coyote saw no reason not to. Perhaps this vermin could actually be of help. But he resolved that, in the future, he would try to avoid questions that the rat would have to answer with words that had s's in them.

"I'm here to find an object of power."

"What kind of power?"

"Power strong enough to break a curse that I put on a prankster of an Indian boy more than a thousand years ago."

"Why do you want to break your curssse?"

"*I* don't want to break my curse, you fool! I want to make sure the *boy* can't break it."

The rat whistled shrilly through the gap.

"A thoussand yearss, you ssay! And he hasn't found an object of power in all that time?"

"No, and I'm going to make sure he never finds it."

Saddam rocked forward onto all fours and sidled up to Coyote.

"I can save you a lot of time," the rat hissed into his ear. "I know the artifactss as well as every millimeter of that pistol. Follow me."

And Saddam led Coyote into a hallway that opened into the Oval Office.

"The boy will come here firsst, mosst likely," said Saddam, "believing it to be the actual office of the Pressident. But issn't. It's a replica. There'ss no power here."

"Then, show me where it is," said Coyote.

Saddam led him back out.

Chapter Three

L ittle Owl was overwhelmed. Artifacts were everywhere. Amazing artifacts. All of which had been handled or written or worn by the Great Chief or the Great Chief's wife or daughters or by other powerful chiefs.

With each step, he saw things that reminded him of events he had heard about during the amazing, sometimes terrifying, years between 2001 and 2009.

How would Little Owl ever find the right object to take him home? To him, every artifact seemed to have more than enough power to overcome Coyote's curse. After all, who was Coyote, compared to the Great Chief?

Little Owl entered the Oval Office. And for a long time, he just stood and stared.

"Ye'll no find what y'r lookin' for in therrre, laddie!" called a distant voice.

Startled, Little Owl tightened his grip on the bow and searched for the source of the disembodied sound.

"D'ye suppose the wee bairn is lost, Uncle Barney?" inquired a sweet, girlish voice.

"Aye, lass, and ah think ah know wha' it'll take t' make him un-lost."

Rounding the corner of a display wall, Little Owl saw bronze statues of two dogs. All at once, the statues disappeared, and before him stood a pair of black Scottish Terriers. Little Owl was more curious than frightened. He sat down on the floor, crossed his legs and laid aside his bow.

"Who are you? What to you know of me?"

"Ma name is Bernard Bush, but everr-one calls me Barney. This bonny lassie is m'niece, Miss Beazley …"

"… named after a great dinosaur," the smaller Scotty interrupted proudly.

Barney cleared his throat.

"Ahem … ah overhearrd a critter talking t' a big, mangy rrat aboot ye just beforre y'entered our fatherr's

18

office, t'uther side o 'the wall."

"Your *father*! exclaimed Little Owl. "The Great Chief is a dog?"

"Ach, dinnae be daft," said Barney.

"We call them father and mother as terms of affection," Miss Beasley explained.

"As the animals on the Red River called me Little Owl instead of Screech Owl," sighed the boy.

The two Scotties cocked their heads as all dogs do when they're trying to understand something.

"Never mind," said Little Owl.

"As Barney began to explain," said a new voice with just the hint of a British accent, "we overheard plans the large fox made with Saddam. And we decided we should find you and even the odds a bit."

And out of a shadow stepped an English Springer Spaniel. She walked gracefully to the boy and held out a regal paw, as she imagined the Queen might do when greeting a commoner.

"My name is Spot Fletcher. You may call me Miss Fletcher. I think Miss Fletcher sounds so much more elegant than 'Spot,' don't you. After all," she whispered, "it isn't my fault that I was named after a *baseball* player. Nevertheless," she sighed, "mother, father and the twins call me Spot. So you might as well do the same. How do you do?"

Little Owl shook her paw, and she turned and sat down beside Miss Beasley.

"Who or what is Saddam?" Little Owl asked.

"He's a rrat!" said Barney with a stronger burr and a growl, "a big, mangy, treacherous rrrat! Dinna ever turn y'r back on him, laddie, ah warn ye."

"What makes you think you can 'even the odds,' as you put it?" asked Little Owl, perhaps not quite as graciously as he might have. "And what makes you think I am not already a match for them both?"

Clearly, his pride was a little wounded that the three dogs seemed to think he was not up to the task of besting Coyote and his scruffy new sidekick.

"We lived with Mom and Dad for years in the White House and had the run of the place," Miss Beasley said, "especially Uncle Barney."

"Ay," interrupted her kinsman, "and we sat in on secret meetings, so we know all there is to know aboot that rrrat."

"We can help you find the artifact you're searching for," Spot said. "You will need all the help you can get, as there are more than three hundred artifacts here in the museum."

"And tens of thousands more downstairs," purred yet another new voice.

"That hearing of hers is gang t'get that lass inta serrious trouble one o' these days," said Barney, shaking his head.

And out of the same shadow that had concealed Spot glided a sleek black cat.

She continued over to Little Owl, rubbed her body along his left thigh, then turned and curled up in front of Miss Beazley.

"My name is India," she said languidly.

"We all call her 'Willie,'" added Spot, who received a dirty look from the cat for his trouble.

Just as Spot preferred to be called Miss Fletcher, India, who also had been named for a baseball player, did not care to have a nickname that rhymed with "silly."

"Are there any more of you?" Little Owl asked.

"One more, perrhaps," said Barney.

21

Spot leaned down to Willie and whispered in her ear, which tickled and made the cat shake her head.

"You go, dear. Perhaps he will listen to you."

"Because we're both cats, you mean."

Spot sensed that she had offended her friend.

"No, dear, because you are much more persuasive than any of us." "*And because*," she thought but did not say, "*he has never tried to eat you.*

Willie licked her paws and washed her face, smoothed her fur and slid back into the shadows.

"Where is she going?" asked the boy.

"To Akili," said Spot.

"Who is Akili?"

"He's a grreat, hulking lion, laddie, sent here from Tanzania as a gift for President Bush."

"I don't believe I've ever seen a lion," said Little Owl. "What's he like?"

"Like Willie," Spot said. "Only much, much bigger and less, well, vain. Akili is very wise, but he keeps mostly to himself. I doubt that he will be joining us."

Little Owl felt a bit relieved, though he didn't say so.

After ten minutes of silence, the dogs began to grow concerned about Willie. Maybe they should not have sent her to Akili alone and unprotected.

Just then, the shadows parted like a curtain, and Willie returned to her place, curled up and said, "He declined." Then, she closed her eyes, sighed and went to sleep.

Since there were far fewer artifacts upstairs than down, Little Owl and Company decided to begin with the more manageable number.

The boy looked on, as the quartet discussed the museum artifacts and shared opinions on which were most likely to suit Little Owl's purposes.

Finally, Barney said, "Therre arr six possibilities. Chances arr verra good that the one y'r lookin' for is one of 'em, and ye'll be home again beforre sunrise."

Focusing their attention on the artifacts, however, they had all forgotten about Coyote and Saddam.

And that was dangerous.

Chapter Four

W illie had suggested that a promising artifact might be found in what the museum staff calls Area Two: Empowering Americans.

One exhibit features a reading room with scores of wonderful children's books recommended by First Lady Laura Bush.

On a table opposite the bookshelves, Willie's life-size bronze statue portrays her curled up with a book, entitled *If You Take a Mouse to the Movies*.

Above the bookshelves, framed posters promote the annual National Book Festivals, established by Mrs. Bush in 2001.

"What is more powerful than education?" Willie asked rhetorically. "Ignorance makes slaves. That's why tyrants kill or imprison educated people and burn books. They know they can't enslave educated people for long."

Everyone agreed that there should be more than enough power in one of the posters to break Coyote's spell. And Little Owl and Company made their way to the reading room.

"This is the one that launched a reading revolution," said Willie, as they gathered in front of a poster that seemed alive with bold, brilliant colors.

"Thirty thousand people attended the first festival," she added. "Twelve years later, there were more than 200,000!"

Anxious to see of this would prove to be the artifact of power, Little Owl stood tiptoe and reached up to touch the poster.

"STOP!" shouted a harsh voice.

The Company turned to find Coyote glaring at them, his eyes squeezed into little yellow slits. Beside him, a big, unwholesome rat crouched, poised to attack.

"We'll take that poster," hissed the rat.

The corners of Little Owl's mouth turned down. His teeth clenched. His muscles tensed. And he tightened his grip on the sturdy wood of his bow.

The others wore similar expressions, even Spot, who could be a formidable foe, despite her pretensions and refinements.

"You might as well relax, all of you," Coyote warned. "The boy and I have met many times on the field of battle—and he has lost every time, is that not so, Little Owl?"

"Only because you cheat, Coyote. And I am not alone this time.

"Nor am I," Coyote growled, furiously.

"Saddam!" Coyote barked, "teach the boy a lesson."

The rat grinned an ugly grin through a food-encrusted beard, his eyes almost invisible behind the puffy bags.

Saddam arched his back, bared his fangs and sprang at Little Owl. But, as he sprang, he noticed his reflection in the glass of the poster frame.

He stopped, dropped to the floor and stood there motionless, mesmerized by his own image.

You see, Saddam was never able to pass any shiny surface without being captured by his reflection. His namesake was the same way. The tyrant of Tikrit loved himself so much that he filled the country with pictures and posters of himself, along with murals and statues and every other kind of representation.

The rat's reveries, however, were interrupted by a

swift kick from Coyote.

But the moment he stopped staring at himself in the glass, Saddam began to recite a poem from *Nonsense Books*, by Edward Lear.

There was a young person of Smyrna,
whose grandmother threatened to burn her,
but she seized on the cat
and said, "Granny, burn that!!
you incongruous old woman of Smyrna!

Another kick, and Saddam shook his head, spun around and was about to resume his attack when a deafening ROARR! Shook the gallery and made the glass in the poster frames rattle and nearly shatter.

Saddam froze.

Coyote spun around to find himself staring into the huge, open mouth of the biggest African lion he had ever seen—in fact, it was the *only* African lion he had ever seen.

Quicker than you can say, "Egad!" Coyote took to his heels, tail between his legs, yelping all the way, as far as he could go, as fast as he could run, never bothering to look back to see if Saddam was close behind, which, in point of fact, he was not.

Saddam remained frozen with fear, like a bushy, mangy, not-at-all-tasty rat sicle.

Akili let out another terrible ROARR! And Saddam fainted. By the time they all had stopped laughing and glanced back to where he had fallen, the rat was gone. No one knew how or when, and no one cared.

Willie glided over to the lion and lifted her face. And Akili lowered his head until their noses touched, as cats do when they greet one another.

"What made you change your mind, Akili?"

"I heard the boy say that the yellow dog uses magic. I came to watch over you."

"Ach, ah wish ye'd no call him a dog, sirrr. He's no kin o'mine. The Prresident was correct aboot Saddam. The hull worrld b'lieved the old Irraqi despot had an army o' doubles t'fool them that were tryin' to kill 'im. M'fatherr used t'joke that Saddam just had multiple personalities. Among otherr things, he thought he was the reincarnation o'Nebuchadnezzarr, King o'Babylon.

He paused, then said with a wink, "It would also seem that he thought himself a bonny poet like Robbie Burns." And everyone enjoyed another healthy laugh at the rat's expense.

Finally, Akili turn to Little Owl.

"Did you find your artifact of power, little one?"

In the commotion, they all had forgotten about their quest.

Little Owl perched again on tiptoe and reached through the protective glass to touch the poster. He ran his finger over the fine paper and ink, as though stroking it might prompt it to respond.

He watched and waited, but nothing happened.

After a couple of minutes, Akili walked up to Little Owl and said gently, "Everything Willie said about education is true, Little Owl. Education is power. But the poster is not education. The poster is art. And art is not the subject itself. Art is an expression, a shadow, an echo or reflection of the subject. It is only an image of a thing perceived or believed or hoped for. It is not the substance, like a prairie sunset or faith in God."

But Little Owl was not discouraged. He had tested many objects throughout the centuries and viewed each, not as another failure, but as another step closer to the one that would set him free.

"What's next?" he asked, rejoining the Company.

"Follow me," said Barney.

Chapter Five

Barney led the Company, including Akili, out of the reading room and around the corner to a display of autographed baseballs.

"This is only a wee parrt of m'father's collection," he told Little Owl. "I think he loves t' chase balls almost as much as we do, though I prefer a soccerr ball or a wee golf ball to one o'these things. Ach, well, t'each his own. Now, read the signatures on th'balls, an' see if anythin' stands out t'ye."

The Company gathered around the display and began to read the signatures. Bo Jackson and the Ripkins—senior, junior and Billy, Whitey Ford, Willie Mays and Micky Mantle. Ted Williams and Joltin' Joe DiMaggio. Some balls with signed by entire teams or Hall of Famers.

Eventually, they found one ball that seemed out of

place. Between Nolan Ryan and Ken Griffey Jr. was a ball autographed by Neil Armstrong and Buzz Aldrin.

"Ay," said Barney, "that's it."

"What is so powerful about a baseball?" Little Owl asked.

"Nae the *baseball*, laddie, the *signatures*. D'ye not know? These men brroke the bonds of Earth. They broke free. D'ye have any idea how much powerr that took? How fast they had to go t'do that? Seven miles a second! Aye, lad, that's twenty-five thousand miles an hourr! Thirty-three times the speed of sound! How much mahr pow'r could y'possibly need to break a wee spell of a curr like Coyote?"

At the mention of Coyote, everyone stopped and looked around. He and Saddam were nowhere to be found.

"We've seen the back of hose two f'r th'last time, ah think. They'll no want t'encounter the likes of Akili again. Dinna worrry, laddie, y'r almost home."

But Coyote had not given up that easily. He had run because Akili caught him by surprise, and he had never seen a lion before. But he was determined that it would not happen again.

Coyote leaned against a wall that bore the names of nearly 3,000 men, women and children who were killed when Islamic terrorists hijacked four passenger airliners on September 11, 2001 and crashed them into the World Trade Center towers in New York, the Pentagon building in Washington and a field near Shanksville, Pennsylvania.

He watched amused as Saddam scurried up and down and hauled and huffed and puffed and whined and was repeatedly shushed.

Coyote delighted in his own cleverness and smiled a sly smile as he considered how stupid Saddam was and how effortlessly he was able to manipulate the rat.

"I was right about the power in that pistol," he thought. "*Rat Power*." Then, he snickered a not very nice snicker.

Soon, their work done, Coyote left with the panting Saddam in search of more mischief.

Akili knew they had not seen the last of Coyote and his parasitic pal, but he said nothing. He stood quietly and watched as Little Owl reached into the display case and touched the ball.

A jolt, like electricity, ran up one of the boy's arms and down the other, down both legs to his toes and up his neck, until his ears popped.

But this artifact wasn't powerful enough, either, to do the job. Little Owl was still in the museum—far away from his village on the Red River with his parents and brothers and sisters, the bighorn ship and puma and peccary, the kangaroo rat, skink and hare, the alligator and the armadillo.

The good news was that he was still with Barney and Miss Beazley, Spot and Willie and Akili. And that gave him hope.

Little Owl shook himself all over and turned—quite naturally, it seemed to him—to Akili for an answer.

"Just as the book festival poster was not education," said the lion, "the baseball is not Apollo 11, nor is it the astronauts who walked on the moon. It is just a baseball. And a baseball is not free. Though it soars all over the stadium, it can go only where it is thrown or hit. Freedom is not the power to soar. Freedom is the ability to choose."

"Excuse me," said Spot, "but I think we have overlooked the most obvious power artifact in the whole building.

And the Company followed her into the next area.

Chapter Six

It was darker here. Little Owl and Company found themselves speaking in whispers, though they would not have been able to tell you why.

In the center of the area was a low, round Plexiglas barrier. Inside the barrier was …. nothing.

"I don't understand," said Spot. "There was a huge piece of mangled steel hanging from the ceiling."

And, indeed, a twenty-two foot steal beam that had been part of the outer wall of the World Trade Center had completely vanished.

They all knew the disappearance had something to do with Coyote and Saddam. But how could the pair have removed such a massive, heavy artifact? How could they have carried it? And where could they possibly hope to hide it?

They thought.

And they thought.

And they thought some more. The dogs cocked their heads. And Willie curled up and went to sleep, perchance to dream of a solution.

Now and again, they all looked up at Akili, hoping the wise lion would give them the answer. But he too had merely laid down and napped.

"I remember a story," Little Owl said.

And when he spoke, everyone but Akili nearly jumped out of their skins, because the area had been so quiet.

They settled down and gathered around him, and the boy continued.

"It was a story my father used to tell about Coyote. Coyote did not always have his mystical, magical powers. In fact, when he was just a cub, he had none at all. He couldn't cast spells or travel through time or appear and disappear whenever he wanted to. All of these powers and others had to be developed, just as my brothers and I had to learn to hunt and fish.

"In the meantime, Coyote's mother wove a Blanket of Invisibility for him, so he could practice sneaking up on people and small animals without being seen.

Little Owl paused. And thought.

"*I wonder …*" he said to himself.

He climbed inside the Plexiglas barrier, grabbed what appeared to be a handful of air and shook it.

Everyone watched, amazed as the air inside the enclosure began to shimmer, from floor to ceiling, like air above hot desert sands.

Little Owl shook harder, and it became a total blur, so no one could see through to the other side.

All at once, the boy jumped up and appeared to climb, hand over hand, toward the ceiling—reaching and grabbing hold of … nothing!

Just below the ceiling, where sturdy steel cables appeared to hang loose, Little Owl stopped and began to untie invisible knots.

Suddenly, from top to bottom, a huge beam of twisted steel appeared, as the grinning Indian boy looked down at his friends.

The beam had been there all the time, invisible inside the blanket Coyote's mother had woven for him and which he had conjured to the museum to deceive Little Owl.

"It's a memorial to all those people over there," Spot said, pointing back to the wall. "On the day of the attack,

British Prime Minister Tony Blair declared:

This mass terrorism is the new evil in our world today. It is perpetrated by fanatics who are utterly indifferent to the sanctity of life and we, the democracies of this world, are going to have to come together and fight it together and eradicate this evil completely from our world.

As she spoke, Little Owl and Company saw a Spot they had never seen before. There was strength and resolve, reminiscent of Prince Hal at Agincourt and Nelson at Trafalgar. But she looked sad as well.

"You climbed down the beam," she said to Little Owl.

"Yes."

"You touched it, you climbed down it."

"Yes, I found it. It was hidden inside Coyote's blanket of invisibility."

"You don't understand," she insisted. "You touched it, and nothing happened. You are still here. I thought for certain ..."

"Hundreds of thousands of visitors have touched the

beam, dear Miss Fletcher," Akili said gently. "As the label says, the beam is a memorial. A reminder that has the power to cause us to weep, to recall lost loved ones, to enrage us against a cowardly enemy that slaughters innocent people in the name of its god. But the deity of such men who do such things is a demon, not a god."

The lion turned away.

"Our world has too many such memorials," he said to the names on the wall, almost groaning. The Holocaust. The Soviet famine. Armenia. Cambodia. Rwanda. Each declares, 'Never again.' But none has sufficient power to prevent another."

Akili wept.

Chapter Seven

Though Willie had been Miss Beazley's chief playmate in the White House, she had played with Barney as well, running and rolling around and nipping at him. But she always deferred to him, because he was her uncle and the darling of 1600 Pennsylvania Avenue, with his own webpage and the starring role in a collection of "Barney Cam" videos that continue to delight adults and children alike who visit the White House.

But now Miss Beazley felt the need to step out of her uncle's shadow. She had an idea she was certain would restore Little Owl to his family and his beloved village on the Red River

"This way," she said excitedly, leading the Company through the exhibits, her tail wagging like a metronome set to prestissimo.

"Just over here."

She headed for a display case that contained three artifacts: a letter, a badge and a Bible.

"It's going to be one of these two," she said, looking at the badge and the Bible. I just know it."

They all glanced back for conformation from Akili, who walked beside Little Owl. But his expression remained inscrutable.

Then, just as they stepped up to the display case, there was a CLICK, a SQUEAK and a THUD, and they dropped into the museum archives below.

But not all of them.

Coyote and Saddam had made the opening too small. And Little Owl and Akili stood watching through the smoothly-cut hole as their friends disappeared and landed with a corporate, "OOF!"

Then, somewhere, way down deep and far away, they heard faintly:

> So they both went slowly down
> and walked about the town
> with a cheerful bumpy sound
> as they toddled round and round.

And everybody cried,

as they hastened to their side,

"See! The Table and the Chair

have come out to take the air.

A few moments later, a familiar voice scolded: "Get away from that mirror!"

Little Owl and Akili stepped back from the edge.

"Why didn't you kill Coyote and the rat back in the reading room?" The boy asked the lion, accusingly. "Then they wouldn't have been able to cause all this mischief."

"I am here only to protect you, if I am needed," Akili explained. "I am not here to remove your enemies or solve your problems, Little Owl. You and your friends are capable of doing that for yourselves."

Little Owl took a deep breath and sighed.

"You have known that each of the artifacts we tried were the wrong ones and why," said the boy. "Do you also know which is the right one?"

"Not yet. But I believe I will recognize it when you find it.

The two friends moved around the trap door and

stood before the display case. Little Owl reached in, touched the badge and read the card:

Badge #1012 had belonged to Officer George Howard, who worked at the emergency Service Unit he had helped establish at John F Kennedy International Airport.

Even though he was off duty, he rushed to the World Trade Center, just as he had done when it was bombed in 1993. This time, however, Officer Howard died trying to save others.

"He always did that," his mother said. "He heard about it and called up and said, 'I'm on my way.'"

Arlene Howard gave her son's badge to President Bush when he met with family of missing firefighters and police officers at Ground Zero.

From that day on, the President carried that badge with him, even after he left the White House. It meant so much to him that he did not give it up until just before the museum was about to open. Despite its importance to him personally, President Bush wanted the American people to be able to see the badge in order to help honor the heroes of that terrible day.

"I have heard Officer Howard's story many times," Akili said, after Little Owl found that the badge would not send him home. "And every time, it speaks of his courage. But I think he was more than courageous. I believe he was a man of tremendous compassion, which is even greater. The kind of power you seek, Little Owl, was in Officer Howard's life, not in his death or in the badge that represented the authority and trust that had been placed in him."

Down below, among the bulk of the artifacts, the rest of the Company found themselves surrounded by boxes and folders, crates, cameras and computers. White cotton gloves on tables. Precious gifts given to the President and his wife by potentates and gifts that were precious in other ways that had been sent to the First Family by Americans from all walks of life.

Over there was a zebra skin that made the all of them shudder. And here was a stuffed leopard that had accompanied Akili to America but which remained in the archives instead of upstairs in the museum.

Willie approached the big cat and lifted her face.

The leopard lowered her head until their noses touched.

"My name is Badriya," she said. "I heard you fall into the boxes. Are you hurt?" They were not. And they told Badriya about Little Owl and Coyote and Saddam and their quest for an artifact powerful enough to return the boy to his family and his village on the Red River.

"If Akili is with you," Badriya assured them, "you will find your artifact. He is very wise. And since he did not lead you down here, he must sense that it lies in the museum.

"Since you cannot return the way you came," she said with a giggle, "I will lead you to the elevator."

The Company followed Badriya through the aisles and nearly ran into her when she stopped suddenly and made a face.

"HEE-yo ha-ROO-foo mm-BY-yah ya ra-FEE-kee!" she growled, which is Swahili for, *that stinks*. "Something evil has been here. We must be careful."

Indeed, something evil had passed that way shortly before they arrived. But it wasn't "some*thing*," it was "some*one*" in the form of Coyote and the rat. Angry that their trap had failed, they had returned to the museum.

There was a grand reunion as Barney and Miss Beazley, Spot and Willie rejoined Little Owl and Akili.

"Coyote and Saddam are back again somewhere," Spot told them. "Badriya came across their trail going to the elevator."

"You saw Badriya?" Akili asked. "Is she well? I could tell you many tales about that one," he said with a twinkle in his soft brown eyes.

"Aye, she's well," said Barney. "She told us aboot some of her adventures among th'arrtifacts. But therr was'na time to hear them all."

"We want to go back down to talk with her more after Little Owl finds his way home," Miss Beazley added, "and you must come with us."

"What about you," asked Willie. "Any luck with the badge or the Bible?"

"Not with the badge," Little Owl said. "If only its owner were here, Akili is sure the power of his compassion would be strong enough to return me to my village. We haven't tried the Bible yet."

He turned to Akili.

"Do I need to try every artifact? You already know whether the Bible will work, don't you?"

"I do. But you do not. You must 'try or die,' as you pledged long ago."

The label identified the artifact as:

The personal Bible of President George W. Bush, read daily while living in the White House. President Bush drew on his strong faith in God and a deeply held set of principles to sustain him during his time in office.

"So this is the source of power of the Great Chief," thought Little Owl.

His hand trembled as he reached into the display case and placed it on the worn cover. And for a while, he held it there. Straining to feel warmth. A tingle. A tremor. But there was nothing.

Little Owl turned to Akili.

"My people learned much about the Bible from missionaries," the lion said. And he explained how prides of lions had listened to them in the darkness outside camps and villages.

"Our ancestors gained great wisdom and taught their cubs. We have passed it along through the generations in awe that Man was chosen by God to receive such great truths."

Then, as though reciting mysterious ancient lore, he spoke the words of Romans 8: "For generations we have waited in eager expectation for the sons of God to be revealed. For we were subjected to frustration, not by our own choice, but by the will of the one who subjected it, in hope that we will be liberated from our bondage to decay and brought into the glorious freedom of the children of God."

Little Owl wondered at the meaning of his words, which were like nothing else the lion had ever told him. But Barney and Miss Beazley and Willie and Spot appeared to understand.

"Many people," said the lion, "treat the Bible as if it were an amulet to ward off evil. It does indeed contain the power to defeat evil, but demons are not afraid of a book. It is only leather and paper. They do not shrink from it like mythical vampires from a crucifix. It is not good luck to have a Bible in the house. Nor is it filled with spells and charms to heal, accumulate wealth or case out demons.

"The Bible is not magical. The Bible is the Word of

God, while magic is merely a manipulation of things God created out of nothing."

Little Owl sat down. He was very tired. After all, he had been at his quest for more than a thousand years.

I would be tired, too. Wouldn't you?

"Dinna give up, laddie," said Barney, sitting beside the boy. "Therre's still one more t'go. And if it's not the one, we'll rest 'til tomorrow night and begin agin, in th'archives."

Chapter Eight

Y ou're the one who lives here," snapped Coyote, "so show me the best place to hide it."
It was true that Saddam had resided in the museum since it opened, but most of the time he had been trapped inside a pistol. Nevertheless, to avoid another scolding, he thought carefully about the places he had seen since his release.

In a display case opposite the badge and the Bible, on the other side of the door leading into the Oval Office, an artifact label read:

Texas Flag Patch. On June 28, 2005, four U.S. Navy SEALs fought over 50 Taliban fighters in the mountains of Afghanistan. Three perished. Texan Marcus Luttrell, the lone survivor, sent the President this patch. On July 18, 2006, President

Bush awarded Petty Officer Luttrell the Navy Cross.

The patch, however, was gone. Willie leapt into the display case and felt around for an invisible blanket.

"It's not there," Little said. "Coyote's not foolish enough to try the same trick twice. He's stolen it and hidden it."

Spot laid down with her chin in her paws.

"It's small and flat and tucked away somewhere in 44,000 square feet of museum space," she sighed. "Even if we divided it up among us, it would take forever."

"But Coyote and Saddam don't know *all* of the hiding places, just *some* of them," said Miss Beazley.

"That's rright, lass!" Exclaimed Barney. "And Coyote has'na been herre lang enough to know aboot many."

"You don't think he would trust Saddam to hide it, do you?" Little Owl asked.

"He might. Let's put ar'sels in place of the rrat."

They all made a face. And Spot, Willie and Miss Beazley said, "Eeeuuu" in unison.

"Uncle Barney," Miss Beazley said, "what else did our dad say about Saddam Hussein?"

Barney sat for a few moments, thinking hard.

"Weel, ah hearrd he had a closet filled with bulletproof hats, b'cause he was afrraid of everrbody … 'cept the Christians he surrounded himself with. He believed they wouldn't try t'assassinate 'im."

"Germaphobe!" Barney said suddenly.

At that, everyone except Akili and Little Owl cocked their heads.

"He was afraid of Germans?" Willie asked.

"Nay, lass, he was afrraid o'germs!"

"I remember that too. Our dad said if he got the slightest scratch, he summoned a flock of physicians. He made people kiss his arms, never his face."

"And he was obsessed with body odor," added Miss Beasley, "scrubbing and bathing all the time and making visitors shower before meeting with him."

Everyone was silent for a moment. Then, they all looked at one another exclaimed, "Men's room!" And they ran out of the gallery, into Freedom Hall, through Freedom Plaza, past the gift shop and into the empty restroom—the most perfect place for a narcissistic, dissociative germaphobe.

Plenty of soap and water. Sanitary blow driers. And

acoustics that make everybody sound great when they sing in the shower … or recite poetry.

But there seemed to be no place to hide anything.

The maintenance crew kept the place spotless.

Maintenance?

Little Owl flew at the door beside the exit and swung it open. And everybody began removing buckets and brooms, soap containers, mops and rolls of tissue. They stripped the shelves and searched the corners, until only one object remained.

Occupying most of the space in the maintenance close was a big automatic floor scrubber, which Little Owl began to dismantle.

And there, inside the battery cover, was the patch— still blood spattered, battle scarred and burned from the blast of a rocket propelled grenade.

Everyone there, except Little Owl, had listened in awe when Marcus Luttrell had visited the Presidential Center and shared the amazing story of the operation that took the lives of his best friend, Lieutenant Michael P. Murphy, and petty officers Matthew Axelson and Danny Dietz. Even exploits passed on by the Caddo elders had never spoken of such faith and courage.

Little Owl held the patch in his hand and waited.

But once again, nothing happened.

"Like Officer Howard's badge," Akili said, "the power of the patch is the power of the man who wore it. But the power of a Navy SEAL is its team, not a single member, no matter how strong and highly trained the man may be. SEAL missions are always accomplished by teams.

"Trust your team, Little Owl. They will help you accomplish your mission."

It was true that no one was giving up, and it was true that every day brought new hope. But now, instead of a few hundred artifacts, they would have to work their way through thousands. And as Spot had said, that would take forever.

Chapter Nine

L ittle Owl and Company separated for the night. Willie returned to her table in the children's reading area. Barney, Miss Beazley and Spot resumed their places atop the computers in the White House living area. Akili proceeded to his accustomed post in front of the Liberty Wall. And Little Owl curled up on a padded bench in the theater that played and replayed *A Charge to Keep*.

He had just fallen asleep when …

"Pssst!"

Little Owl was exhausted and had already begun to dream.

"Pssst! Little Owl! Wake UP!"

The boy twitched and opened his eyes. Then yawned. Then stretched. My goodness, you would have thought he had been asleep for hours.

"What do you know about God?" Willie asked, shaking him a little to get him to pay attention to her.

Little Owl cocked his head, then stood and rubbed his eyes.

"He is called KAH-dee AH-yoh," he said.

"What is he like?"

"He is the Sky Chief. The Chief Above All. He gives us game and rain and sun and harvest.

"He is your Provider?"

"Yes."

"Do you think he knew that you were going to trick Coyote?"

Little Owl thought for a moment. Surely, Caddi Ayo had seen Coyote steal his porridge many times. And surely he had seen Little Owl pick the green ground cherries and put them into the porridge.

"Yes."

"And did he know that Coyote would put a spell on you?"

"He knows Coyote, so he must have."

"And he provided you with a bow."

"Yes."

"But if Caddi Ayo is your Provider, wouldn't he also have provided you with arrows?"

"He did, but I couldn't reach them in time."

"Then, he might provide you with arrows *here*, mightn't he?"

"The ARROW!" Shouted Barney, Miss Beazley and Spot, for they had heard Willie slip from her reading room into the theater and were listening in the doorway, as was Akili.

You would have thought someone had fired a starting pistol at a racetrack. They all took off running together, their claws clicking on the polished limestone floor and causing them to slip and slide and careen into one another.

Deep inside the museum, the two words echoed to the sharp ears of Coyote and Saddam.

"The ARROW!"

And they too started running just as fast as they could go, rounding the corner just as Little Owl and Company arrived.

Chapter Ten

In the same display that held Saddam's Glock was a narrow wooden box. Inside the box was a long, wooden arrow, described as:

> The arrow presented to President Bush by Prime Minister Koisumi at the Asia Pacific Economic Cooperation Summit, on October 20, 2001.

The presentation box's message, inscribed by the prime minister reads,

> "The arrow to defeat evil and bring peace on earth."

It was a very special arrow, a whistling arrow used

by ancient Japanese warriors on horseback as they headed into battle. They believed the whistling would chase away evil spirits.

Perfect!

Little Owl and Coyote reached the case together.

For a moment, they stopped and looked at each other. Then, both dove into the display case and grabbed for the arrow.

This time, Little Owl did not come out with a fistful of grass.

This time, he gripped an arrow.

Quick, like a rabbit, he nocked the arrow to his bowstring and turned to face Coyote.

Coyote shouted something that rhymed and seemed to be a command …. but nothing happened.

He shouted again.

He recited a whole anthology of rhymes and spells, curses and incantations …

But nothing happened.

Nor did grasping the arrow return little Owl to his village. But the boy wasn't thinking about that just now. His big brown eyes were strong and hard like the *bois de arc* wood from which the Caddo made their bows.

Coyote spun around and took to his heels

But this time, he was not pursuing Little Owl. He was fleeing from him.

Little Owl drew the bowstring to his eye and sighted along the shaft.

Coyote ran faster than he had ever run in his life. He ran so fast he thought his lungs would burst. He slipped and skid on the limestone and was just about to turn a corner when, TWANG!

Little Owl sent "the arrow to defeat evil" whistling, straight and sure to its target.

Suddenly, lots of things happened all at once.

Coyote howled, grabbed his rump and disappeared, the howl becoming a wail and fading away through time.

The arrow dropped to the floor and, as it did, the museum was filled with the roar of a mighty, swirling wind. The vortex sucked Saddam, screaming, back into the dull, black pistol in the display case.

At the same time, it surrounded Little Owl like a cocoon and lifted him gently from the floor.

It was calm inside the vortex, as in the eye of a hurricane. And it glowed with a wonderful light that Little Owl could actually feel and that made the boy wonder if this was what it was like to be hugged by Caddi Ayo.

The air inside the vortex smelled like woods and grass and roasted game, aromas that reminded him of his village on the Red River.

And he knew he was going home.

Far above, voices grew nearer and clearer. The voices of his mother and father and brothers and sisters. They were laughing and crying and calling his name.

He also heard the familiar voices of the bighorn sheep and puma and peccary, the kangaroo rat, skink and hare, the alligator and the armadillo.

And down below, Little Owl heard the barks and meows of his new friends, and a great, triumphant ROAR! that made him want to jump down and hug the lion and rumple his mane and roll around and wrestle with Willie and the dogs.

It was still dark the following morning when night security guards went home and the day shift assumed their posts.

The lights blinked on. Video screens throughout the museum resumed telling their stories.

The first docents arrived just after eight, had their team meeting, grabbed their walk-talkies and moved through the museum to their assigned areas.

And at nine, sharp, the first visitors passed through the metal detector.

Ann, one of the docents who had begun serving at the museum months before it opened, was assigned to Area 5: Living in the White House. It would be a while before any visitors reached her section, so she browsed the exhibits and read the documents and artifact labels as she always did, trying to learn something new on every shift.

Ann also had a habit, when she was quite alone, of talking to the bronze statues of the Bush dogs (she talked to Willie's statue when she worked in Area 2). She would even pet them, though they weren't furry and fluffy and playful like the real Barney, Miss Beazley and Spot.

This morning, however, she noticed that something looked different.

Ann couldn't put her finger on it at first.

It seemed to her that the statues had been moved. Ever so slightly. But they had definitely been moved.

"John," she said into the walkie talkie. "This is Ann in Area 5. I know this is going to sound crazy, but I think somebody moved the dog sculptures."

"I wouldn't say 'crazy,' Ann" replied the docent team coach, "just 'impossible.' The sculptures are secured to their bases. They can't be moved."

"Of course, you're right, John," she said. "Just an early morning senior moment."

And she clicked off.

Ann stepped out of her area and gazed down through areas 4 and 6. No visitors yet.

Then, she returned to the sculptures, set down her walkie-talkie and gave Barney a good shove.

He was immovable.

And yet ... Ann thought.

About the author

Author of the international best-seller, S*on of Hamas*, Ron Brackin has traveled extensively in the Middle East as an investigative journalist. He was in the West Bank and Gaza during the Al Aqsa Intifada, in Baghdad and Mosul after the fall of Iraq and with the rebels and refugees of southern Sudan and Darfur.

He served as a U.S. congressional press secretary during the Reagan Administration, as a broadcast journalist with WTOP-AM, formerly the all-news CBS radio station in Washington, D.C. and as weekend news anchor for Metromedia's WASH-FM.

Ron has contributed articles and columns to *USA Today*, *The Washington Times* and other publications.